Can YOU spot Oisín's
Evil Twin hidden in the story?

For my beloved baby daughter, Danu.
One of a kind.

Oisín McGann began writing and illustrating stories when he was about six or seven. His spelling wasn't very good and he copied other stories a lot. And he only ever drew weird stuff. As he got older, he got better at spelling and making up his own ideas and drawing ordinary things. He worked in a bunch of places where they didn't want him making up ideas or drawing weird stuff. They told him to grow up and stop being silly.

So he left those jobs and now he writes and draws for a living. He says anyone can do it, if they really want to.

Oisín has made up more stuff about Lenny and his grandad in **Mad Grandad's Flying Saucer, Mad Grandad's Robot Garden, Mad Grandad and the Mutant River, Mad Grandad and the Kleptoes** and **Mad Grandad's Wicked Pictures**.

Mad Grandad's
DOPPELGANGER

Oisín McGann

THE O'BRIEN PRESS
DUBLIN

First published 2010 by The O'Brien Press Ltd,
12 Terenure Road East, Rathgar, Dublin 6, Ireland.
Tel: +353 1 4923333; Fax: +353 1 4922777
E-mail: books@obrien.ie
Website: www.obrien.ie

ISBN: 978-1-84717-197-9

A catalogue record for this title is available from
the British Library.

1 2 3 4 5 6 7 8 9 10
10 11 12 13 14

The O'Brien Press
receives assistance from

Layout and design: The O'Brien Press Ltd.
Illustrations: Oisín McGann
Printed and bound by M&A Thomson Litho Ltd.
The paper in this book is produced using pulp from
managed forests.

CHAPTER 1

Far into the Car Park

It was Saturday morning and I was helping Grandad look for his car. It wasn't stolen. We had **lost** it at the shopping centre. We came out of the cinema and found ourselves in the huge, huge car park. We couldn't see the car anywhere.

We looked around in the rain for nearly an hour and then came back in. Grandad shook the water off his umbrella.

'It's no good, Lenny,' he said. 'We need help.'

'Why don't we stick up some **posters**, Grandad?' I said.

'Great idea!' Grandad replied.

We went into a photocopy shop and told the girl at the counter what we wanted. Grandad gave her a photo of his car. She **scanned** it onto the computer.

Now, you might wonder why Grandad kept a photo of his car in his wallet. You see, Grandad was a bit mad. He thought that **trees** whispered to him, or that his **shoes** took him places he didn't want to go.

Sometimes he even forgot what his car looked like. So he always kept a **photo** with him.

The girl at the counter did up the poster and showed it to us.

'Perfect!' said Grandad. 'We'll take a hundred copies, please. And some tape.'

MISSING
Old Red Car Lost In Car Park

Slightly Rusty with Surprised-Looking Headlights. Spare Set of False Teeth Left on Ba... ...t ...n Reward Offered F... ...t Please Call 087...

'The rolls of tape are down beside that big **cupboard**,' the girl said.

Grandad walked to the end of the shop and the girl went to make the copies.

I gazed out the window at the rain. When I looked round again, Grandad was standing there waiting for me, holding the box of posters.

'Wow! That was **quick**!' I said. 'Where's the girl gone?'

'Oh, she had stuff to do,' Grandad replied. 'Come on, let's go put up these posters.'

CHAPTER 2

Grandad's Dodgy Goggles

We walked around outside, sticking up the posters. It was very wet, but I held the umbrella over Grandad as he stuck them up.

I kept looking at him. There was something **strange** about him, but I couldn't work out what. Then I got it.

'Grandad!' I said. 'Your glasses are different. They're **round** instead of square!'

'Really?' he gasped.

He took them off and looked at them.

'You're right, Lenny!' he said. 'I ... I must have put these old **round** goggles on by mistake. Hang on a second ...'

He spun round for a few seconds
and then turned back to look at me
through his normal, **square** glasses.

'That's better,' he said. 'Come on, let's walk into town. We can put some posters up there. And it'll be harder for someone to **follow** us in town.'

'Who's following us?' I asked.

'Oh, nobody,' he replied.

I'd never seen Grandad wearing round glasses before. He did have loads of old pairs. And who could be following us? I thought it was all a bit **odd**.

We started up the street,
putting up posters as we went.
The rain stopped and I took down
the umbrella. That was when I
noticed something **else** that was
strange about Grandad.

'Hey, Grandad,' I said to him. 'How come you're so **thin**?'

'Eh?' he said. Then he looked down at himself and gave a little yelp. 'Oh! It's just the way my trousers are hanging, Lenny.'

He gave himself a little **shake** and jumped around a bit.

'There, see?' he said, doing another little twirl.

It was true, he did look chubbier now. But I was sure you couldn't look thinner or fatter because your trousers hung the wrong way. Something was **definitely** wrong with Grandad.

CHAPTER 3

The Full Head of Hair

Grandad said we should put up some posters in the **market** in the town square.

'But that's **miles** from the shopping centre,' I said to him.

'Yes, but there's loads of people around,' he told me. 'And we'll be harder to find.'

'Who are we hiding from?' I asked.

'Oh, nobody,' he said.

There were **loads** of stalls in the market, selling all sorts of stuff.

'There are so many different things here,' Grandad chuckled. 'I love when things aren't all the **same**, don't you?'

'Sure,' I said.

I was getting worried now.
Grandad was acting strange. I mean,
he acted strange all the time, but this
was different. He was even **stranger**
than normal.

Then I noticed something else that
was odd about him.

'Grandad, how come your hair's
grown back?' I asked.

'Eh?' he grunted, feeling the top of his head.

All my life, Grandad had been **bald**. Now he had a full head of hair.

'What's going on?' I shouted. 'Who are you and what have you done with my grandad?'

'But I am your grandad!' he cried.

'MY GRANDAD IS **BALD**!' I yelled, and I started hitting him with the umbrella. 'MY GRANDAD HAS NO HAIR!'

'Ouch! Ouch!' yelled Grandad
as he tried to dodge the umbrella.

People were starting to look at us. Grandad just smiled and shrugged at them.

'Okay, okay!' he whispered then. 'I'll tell you everything. Please stop **hitting** me!'

CHAPTER 4

Ditto the Doppelganger

The fake Grandad led me into a big secondhand shop. I left the wet umbrella by the door.

The woman at the counter was reading a newspaper and didn't take any notice of us. It was a good thing too, because just then ...

... Grandad did something really, really **strange** indeed.

He **changed** into someone else. One minute he was Grandad; the next minute he looked like the girl from the photocopy shop ... but **different**. She looked kind of the same, but with more tentacles and stuff. She seemed a bit sad and scared.

'I'm a **doppelganger**,' she told me. 'I can make myself look like just about anybody. My brother Dupe and I pretend to be other people so we can use their stuff and hang out with their friends.'

'That's really **sneaky**,' I told her, with an angry scowl. 'You should get your own friends. Where's my grandad?'

'I'll take you to him,' she said, 'but I need to explain on the way.'

She made herself look a bit more **normal** so people wouldn't stare.

As we headed back to the photocopy shop, she told me everything. She said her name was Ditto. She and her brother Dupe weren't talking to each other because of a big **argument**. Now she was really lonely.

She'd seen the way me and Grandad got on so well. So when we came into her shop, she pushed Grandad into a cupboard and made herself look like him so that I could be her **friend**.

It was really annoying, but I felt a bit sorry for her.

'Now I think Dupe is following me,' she said. 'He's not very good at copying people, but he can make himself look like any kind of **object**. The only parts of him he can't change are his **eyes**.

He can't stand to look at himself. And he hates it when people can see him. He'd make you disappear **forever** if you saw him!'

It started **raining** again. I picked up the umbrella and put it up.

'Don't worry,' I said. 'We'll watch out for him.'

CHAPTER 5

Grandad Gets Mad

We got back to the shop and let
Grandad out of the cupboard. He was
angry with Ditto, but when he heard
her story, he felt **sorry** for her too.

'That's no way to make friends, young lady!' he said.

'I know,' she replied, looking very ashamed. 'I'm really sorry. And Dupe will be so **jealous** that I've been talking to you!

'Nobody's supposed to see what **doppelgangers** really look like. He could drag you into our world – make you disappear forever. He can do that, you know … '

'He won't be dragging us **anywhere**,' said Grandad. 'I know just how to catch him out.'

It was still raining when me and Grandad walked out of the shop. He put up the umbrella again. We walked down some steps that led to the car park.

Suddenly the umbrella jumped out of Grandad's hand. It started changing shape, growing into a savage **creature**. It looked like Ditto, but was much, much bigger.

It was **Dupe**. He bared his snaggly
teeth at us and grabbed hold of us.

'You stole my sister!' he snarled.
'I'm going to make you disappear.
Nobody will ever see you two again!'

Dupe pulled out a big **bag**
and was about to stuff us inside.

CHAPTER 6

Stopping the Copying Doppelganger

Suddenly, Grandad started to change too! His **shape** wobbled and warped until he looked exactly like Dupe.

The doppelganger gave out a yelp and stumbled back, covering his eyes. He couldn't bear to look at himself.

'Arrgh!' he squealed. 'How are you are doing that? **Stop** it!'

It wasn't Grandad, of course. It was **Ditto** – pretending to be Grandad! And now she was making herself look like Dupe.

As Dupe wailed and covered his eyes, the real Grandad jumped out from behind a van.

He pulled out a roll of **sticky tape**, and Ditto helped hold her brother while Grandad whipped the tape around his arms and legs. In seconds, the nasty doppelganger was all wrapped up, stuck in his real shape.

Ditto turned back to her normal shape too.

'We're going to stop making copies of people,' she told her brother. 'It's not right. And I want to be **myself**, not someone else.'

'Listen to your sister, lad,'
Grandad growled. 'Any more
nonsense from you and I'll ... I'll
stick your face to a **mirror**.'

Dupe gave a scared little whimper and stared up at his sister, looking really **miserable**.

'I wasn't really going to hurt anyone,' he sobbed. 'I was just **lonely**. I'm not good at doing things on my own.'

'Then maybe you can do stuff with us sometimes,' Grandad told him. 'Just so long as you stop being so **sneaky**.'

The two doppelgangers looked very happy with that.

I was already wondering if
Dupe could turn into a quad bike
or a **submarine** ...

The doppelgangers helped us find Grandad's **car** and then we drove home.

We do hang out with them
sometimes. They are doing proper
work in the photocopy shop and
have their **own** lives now.

But there might still be more of the sneaky ones out there, so remember – keep an eye out for those **eyes**!